This is my book.
My name is

....

Will you please read to me?

Thank you.

The Beginner's Bible
Tales of Virtue: A Book of Right and Wrong

Library of Congress Catalog Card Number: 94-74176
ISBN: 679-87637-5

Manufactured in the United States of America

First Edition: March 1995

TALES of VIRTUE

A Book of Right and Wrong

As told by **Carolyn Nabors Baker**
Illustrated by **Kelly Pulley**
and **Lisa Reed**

Note to parents and grandparents:

We know that your child's character development is very important to you. So find a quiet place, take your child in your arms, and come with us through the pages of timeless Bible stories as we unfold ten virtues important for children to learn and treasure.

Each tale first defines a virtue in a way your child can understand. Then, we show how a biblical character from a classic story portrays that virtue. Finally, we encourage your child to apply this virtue to his or her own life. Learning about right and wrong is more fun than ever!

Contents

Forgiveness

Do you know what forgiveness means? When someone does something mean to us, we can choose to be kind to them. That is forgiveness.

Jacob lived in the land of Canaan
with his twelve sons.
He had one son named Joseph.
Joseph was his very favorite.
This made Joseph's brothers very angry.

One day Jacob gave Joseph a new coat.
It had many beautiful colors.
Joseph's brothers were very angry
and jealous.
They wanted new coats too!

One night Joseph had a dream.
The next day he told his brothers
about the dream.
Joseph said, "We were all gathering grain
in the fields. My bundle of grain stood up.
Your bundles of grain bowed down
to mine."
Joseph's brothers did not like his dream.
They did not like Joseph.

Joseph's brothers did mean things to him.
They wanted to get rid of him.
They took his beautiful coat away from
him and sold him to travelers
going to Egypt.
That was mean.
But Joseph forgave them.
Joseph's brothers did not care about him.
But God cared for Joseph!

When Joseph came to Egypt, the people
put him in jail.
Then the king called him, and said,
"I had a strange dream;
what does it mean?"
Joseph said, "There is going to be a
famine in the land."
The king knew Joseph was wise.
The king asked Joseph to help the people
save food.

When the famine came,
Joseph's brothers did not have
enough food.
They said, "We must go to Egypt
and buy food."
When his brothers came, they did not
know who Joseph was.
But Joseph knew who they were.

The brothers bowed down to Joseph and
asked him for some food.
Joseph said, "I will sell you some food."
Then the brothers went back home.

Joseph missed his brothers.
When they needed more food,
they came back to Egypt.
Joseph said to them, "You don't have to
worry about food anymore!
I am your brother. I will help you.
God wanted me to come to Egypt
and be a leader.
He has been kind to me.
Now I want to be kind to you!"

Could you do what Joseph did?
If your brother or sister did mean things
to you, could you be kind to them?
That is what Joseph did.
That is forgiveness.

Loyalty

Loyalty means to stay with someone
in the fun times and
in the sad times.
Loyalty means that we will never
leave our friends when they
need us.

A long time ago Ruth lived with Naomi
in the land of Moab.
Ruth was married to one of Naomi's sons.
Then a sad thing happened.
Naomi's husband died.
Soon Ruth's husband died too.
Ruth and Naomi were all alone.
What would they do?

Naomi wanted to go back to
Bethlehem where she grew up.
She tried to get Ruth to stay in Moab.
Naomi said, "Ruth, stay in Moab.
You can marry again. You can have
a new husband and a home."

Ruth did not want to stay in Moab
without Naomi.
She wanted to go with Naomi.
Ruth said, "I don't ever want to leave you.
I want to stay with you forever."
Ruth loved Naomi very much.

So Ruth and Naomi walked
to Bethlehem together.
The trip was long and hard.
When they came to Bethlehem,
Naomi said, "I'm tired and hungry."
Ruth said, "I will help you. I will work
in the fields and gather grain for us."
She worked all day long
to get enough food.

It was not easy for Ruth
to work in the fields.
It was not easy because she was
from Moab.
The Bethlehem workers might not like
someone they did not know.
But Ruth said, "I am not afraid.
Naomi is too old and tired to work
in the fields. I will be loyal to my friend.
I will take care of her."

Ruth was good to Naomi.
She did not leave Naomi.
She stayed with her and helped her.
Later, Ruth married a man named Boaz.
Even then Ruth said, "I will never leave
you, Naomi."
Naomi was very happy.

You can say to someone near you,
"I will always be here for you in the
happy times and in the sad times.
I will not leave you."
That is loyalty.

Responsibility

Responsibility means to take care
of the things God and others
have given us.

God made the very first man,
and he named him Adam.
Then he made a very beautiful garden.
He called it Eden.
God said to Adam, "This garden
will be your home."
The garden was a wonderful place
for Adam to live.

Everything that Adam needed
to be happy was in the garden.
There were rolling, green fields.
There was a clean, clear river.
There were trees with tasty fruit.
There were trees with colorful flowers.
There were birds singing in the branches
of the trees.
There were animals playing everywhere.
There was a lot of water
to help the plants grow.

Adam said, "God has made a very
beautiful home for me.
I am happy living here."

God wanted Adam to do something
very important.
So God said, "I want you to work
the fields in this garden.
I want you to take care of the river.
I want you to take care of everything
in the garden that I have given you."

God knew that Adam was alone
in the garden of Eden.
He had lots of fun with the birds
and the animals.
But Adam needed someone special
to help him.
Then God said, "I will make a woman
for Adam."
He said, "She can be his friend.
She can be his wife.
She can be his helper."

And God made the first woman and
named her Eve.

Adam and Eve worked together
in the garden.
They helped each other.
They worked in the green fields.
They took good care of everything
God had given them.
Adam said, "I am happy."
Eve said, "I am happy."
God was happy too.

God has given you many things to enjoy.
He wants you to take care
of all the good things he has given you.
That is responsibility.

Friendship

What is friendship?
Friendship is having someone
to play with, and to help, and
to watch over.

Many years ago the very first king
of Israel was King Saul.
His son, the prince, was named Jonathan.
Jonathan had seen David fight
the giant Goliath.
When Jonathan met David, he liked
him and wanted to be his friend.

David played the harp.
When the king wanted to hear good music
he called for David.
Jonathan liked David's music too.
David and Jonathan had fun together.

Jonathan showed David around
the palace.
He showed him his trophy room and
all his trophies and awards.
David had never seen anything
like that before.
Jonathan said, "I would like to give you
my royal sword and my royal robe,
my belt and my bow."
Jonathan and David became best friends
from that time on.
They had fun together, and they always
watched out for each other.

Sometimes King Saul
would get mad at David.
Once he threw his spear at him.
But David jumped out of the way.
Jonathan was afraid the king
would hurt David.
So he said to him, "Tell me what to do
to help you. I will do anything."
They made a promise to each other
and said, "We will be friends forever
and we will always help and watch over
each other."

King Saul still wanted to hurt David.
So Jonathan came to David and said,
"I have a plan. David, you must hide.
I will talk to my father to see if he is still
very angry with you. Then I will come
back and let you know."
So Jonathan came to David and said,
"Even though I want you to stay here
you must run far away and hide
from the king."

David and Jonathan were sad.
They did not want to leave each other.
Then Jonathan said, "Don't worry, David.
We will be best friends forever."
Even though Jonathan and David
were not together,
they would still be best friends.

Friends are very special people.
We help them.
We do good things for them.
We watch over them.
That is what Jonathan did for David.
That is what you can do too!
That is friendship.

Courage

Do you have courage?
Courage is inside everyone.
It comes out when we decide
to stand up for what is right
and good.
It comes out sometimes
when we are most afraid.

Esther lived with her cousin Mordecai
in the land of Persia.
One day the king of Persia decided
to choose a new queen.
He said, "I want Esther to be my queen.
She is the most beautiful woman
in all the land."

Now there was a man named Haman
who did bad things.
Haman said to everyone, "You must kneel
down to me because
I am more important than you."
Mordecai said, "I will not kneel down for
Haman. I will only kneel down for God."
This made Haman very, very mad.
Haman wanted to hurt Mordecai, and
all of Mordecai's people.
So Haman made a plan.

He decided to trick the king.
Haman told the king that Mordecai and
his people were bad.
Haman said to the king, "If you will
make a law to hurt Mordecai and all of
his people, I will give you a lot of money."
Now the king liked money, so he said,
"Yes, I will do this."
They had a feast. Haman was happy.

But when Mordecai heard
of the new law, he cried.
All of Mordecai's people were afraid.
The people did not know what to do.
Mordecai said, "I can help. I will tell my
cousin Queen Esther to talk to the king.
She can ask him not to hurt my people."

At first, Esther was very afraid.
She thought, "I cannot go to the king
unless he calls for me.
I might lose my life."
What would Esther do?
Would she have courage?
Esther made her choice.
She said, "I want to help my people.
I am willing to go to the king."

When Esther went to the king,
he was happy to see her.
Esther told the king about Haman's trick
to hurt Mordecai's people.
She said to the king, "Please save
these good people because they are
my people too!"
The king was surprised.
He said, "I can write a new law.
I will help all of Mordeci's people."

Queen Esther was very happy.
She knew she had done the right thing.
She saved all of Mordecai's people.
She had a lot of courage.

You have courage too.
It is right inside of you.
When someone wants to hurt your friend,
you can say, "No, I will not let you.
I will help my friend."
That is courage.

Obedience

"I need you to do something for
me," your father might say.
You can say to your father,
"I'm too tired.
I don't want to."
But when you choose to do what
your mother or father tells you
to do, that is obedience.

God wanted to help the people
in the great city of Nineveh.
He said to Jonah, "Go and help
these people. Tell them to stop doing
bad things."

At first Jonah would not listen to God.
He didn't want to obey God.
He wanted to do something different.
So he tried to run away from God.

Jonah wanted to get far away
from Nineveh.
He boarded a big boat that was sailing far
away from Nineveh.
But God was watching Jonah.

God sent a storm so big that the boat
almost broke apart.
The sailors were afraid.
They said to Jonah, "Are you the reason
for this bad storm?"
Jonah said to them, "Yes. I am the reason.
But if you throw me into the sea,
it will stop."
So the sailors did what Jonah said.
And the storm went away.

Soon a great fish came up and
swallowed Jonah.
Jonah prayed very hard to God
from inside this fish.
He said, "Please help me. I am sorry."
After three long days and nights,
God saved Jonah.
The great fish spit Jonah out
onto dry land.

Then God said to Jonah again, "Go to
Nineveh and help these people. Tell them
to stop doing bad things."
This time Jonah listened to God.
This time he decided to obey God.
He went to Nineveh and told the people
what God had said.

And the king of this great city said to his
people, "Stop doing bad things and
start loving God."
And the people did.
Hooray! God saved the city of Nineveh.
Jonah obeyed God and God was glad.

When your mother, father, or teacher tells
you to do good things, do you obey
them?
When God tells you good things to do,
do you obey him?
That is what Jonah learned to do.
That is obedience.

Sharing

God shares with us because he
wants to.
He doesn't keep all the good
things for himself.
God shares with us because it
makes him happy.
Sharing with your friends
and family can make
you happy too.

Now there was a king in Israel
named Ahab.
He did many, many evil things.
One day a man of God, named Elijah,
said, "Ahab, because you have done so
many evil things in the land, God will
stop the rain for a long, long time."

God told Elijah to go to a brook
where there would be water.
Elijah said, "Where will I find food?"
God shared food with Elijah when
he sent birds called ravens
that brought him bread.

Soon the brook dried up because
there was no rain.
Elijah said, "Where will I find water?"
And God said to Elijah, "I want you
to go and stay in a small village.
There is a woman who lives there who
will help you."

So Elijah went to this village.
He said to the woman, "I am thirsty.
Please give me a little water."
Elijah was also hungry, so he said
to the woman, "Please give me
a piece of bread too."

And the woman said, "I don't have
any bread.
I have only a little oil and flour left.
I'm going home now to make the last
meal for me and my son."
She knew she didn't have enough
for Elijah.

Elijah said to the woman, "Don't be
afraid. Go home and make a small loaf
of bread for you and your son
and for me.
God has told me that your oil and your
flour will not run out."
So the woman said, "I will do what you
have told me to do."
And she shared all that she had
with Elijah.
She said, "I don't want to keep good
things just to myself."

She was happy to share all that she had
with Elijah.
Elijah knew God would share good
things with her.
And God did.
The woman did not run out of
oil and flour.
There was enough food for her and her
son and Elijah.
The woman was glad she had shared
with Elijah.

You can share too.
When we happily give what we have
to others, that is sharing.
God shares with us, and he is happy
when we share with others.

Patience

What is patience?
It is waiting for God to give us
the things we need
at just the right time.

Many years ago there was a woman
who lived in Judah.
Her name was Hannah.
She didn't have any children.
More than anything in all the world
Hannah wanted to have a son.

Every day Hannah prayed to God.
She said, "I am very sad because I don't
have a son.
Please give me a son."
She waited and waited and waited.
Another woman laughed at Hannah
because she had a son,
and Hannah did not.
Hannah cried and cried and cried.
She was very sad.

Hannah's husband tried to make
Hannah smile.
He said, "Hannah, tell me why
you are so sad."
And Hannah said, "I have no son."

Then one day Hannah said, "I will talk to
God. I will make a promise to him."
She said, "Please give me a son.
If you will give me a son, I will let him
serve you all of his life."

Hannah prayed and prayed
and she waited and waited.
She was still very sad.

One day a man of God named Eli
talked to Hannah.
He said, "Do not worry.
Be patient.
May God give you a son at
the right time."

Hannah was happy.
She knew she would have a son
at the right time.
She knew she did not have
to worry anymore.
There were no more tears in her eyes.
She was not sad anymore.

Hannah said, "I waited on God
and he gave me a son
at just the right time.
I am very thankful to God."

Even when we have to wait,
we can still trust God.
If you are patient, God will give you
what you need at just the right time.
It was hard for Hannah to wait on what
she wanted God to give her.
Hannah was happy that she learned
to be patient.
You can learn to be patient too.

Work

Work is what God or others
give us to do.
When we do our special work
we learn, we grow,
and we are happy.

There once was a good man named Noah.
Noah lived a long, long time ago.
He lived at a time when people began
to do many bad things.
God was very sad because of this,
and he wanted to start all over.
So God said, "I must find a good man
who will do special work for me."
And God found Noah!

God said to Noah, "I am going to send a great flood that will cover all the Earth. I will wash away all of the bad things on the earth and make it new again."

Then God said, "I have special work for
you. I want you to build a very large boat
called an ark, and I will tell you just how
to build it. I will tell you how wide and
how high it needs to be, and I will tell
you what kind of wood to use.
Building the ark will take a very long time
and a lot of hard work.
Will you do this for me, Noah?"
And Noah said, "Yes!"

Noah worked every day on the ark.
He worked for many years.
His sons helped him.
Sometimes it was easy. Sometimes it was
hard. Sometimes it was fun. Sometimes
it was boring.
But they knew they were doing
God's special work.
Noah did everything God told him to do.
He was happy because his work made
his family strong.

Then God said to Noah, "I have some
more work for you to do.
I want you to take every kind of animal
into the ark.
Take food for the animals and for you.
And take your wife and your
whole family too."

Noah did everything that God told
him to do.
Then God closed the door to protect them
from the storm.
Noah was happy to do God's special
work because God kept him and his
family safe and warm inside the ark.

Noah lived on the ark a very long time.
After the flood was over, God brought
Noah and his family and all the animals
to a brand new land.
Noah was happy.
Noah thanked God for choosing him to
do this special work.

God took care of Noah and his family.
God was happy that Noah did
his special work.
God put a rainbow in the sky and
promised never to flood the earth again.
God has special work for us to do.
When we do our special work, we can be
happy too.

Honesty

Honesty means to tell the truth
to ourselves and to others.
God tells the truth.
He is honest.
God wants you to tell the
truth too.

Daniel lived a long time ago
in the land of Babylon.
He was very handsome
and he was very smart.
He was also very healthy.
So the king said, "I want Daniel to work
in the palace."

Daniel went to live in the king's palace.
The king wanted Daniel to eat the food.
But the food was not healthy.
It was too rich.
It was not good for Daniel
to eat the king's food.
Daniel said, "I cannot eat the king's food.
It will make me feel bad.
I want to eat what is healthy for me."
It was hard, but Daniel was honest.
He was even honest with the king.

Later, the king had a dream.
He said to the wise men, "Tell me
what my dream means."
And they said to the king, "We cannot
do what you ask."
And the king was very angry.
He wanted to hurt all of the wise men
in the kingdom.
The king said, "If you cannot tell me what
my dream means, then you
are not wise men."

Now Daniel heard about what
the king said. He prayed in the night that
God would tell him the king's dream and
what it meant. And God did.
Then the king asked Daniel,
"Can you explain my dream?"
Daniel could have said, "I am very wise.
I know what your dream means."
But he did not.
He said, "God has explained your
dream to me."
Daniel was honest.
He told the king the truth.
The king was happy.

Some of the wise men in the kingdom
were jealous of Daniel because
he was so honest.
They could not find anything wrong
with him.
Daniel had never broken the law.
So they thought of a plan to trap Daniel.
They said to the king, "Make a law that
people can only pray to you.
If anyone breaks the new law, throw him
into the lions' den."

Now Daniel heard about this evil plan.
But he did not stop praying to God.
Every day Daniel went to his
room to pray to God.
Daniel was honest and true to God.

The jealous wise men saw Daniel
praying in his room.
They said, "Daniel has broken the king's
new law. Now we can throw
Daniel into the lions' den."
The king was very sad that Daniel
had broken his law.
He liked Daniel, but he could not change
the law.

What would the king do?
The king said, "I hope God will keep
you safe."
And God did. He sent an angel to close
the lions' mouths and to
watch over Daniel. Daniel was saved!
The king was happy.
Daniel was glad that he had prayed
to God.
Daniel was glad that he had been honest.

Daniel wanted to be honest
because he loved God.
When you are honest, this makes
God happy.
God took care of Daniel.
God will take care of you.

ALSO FROM LITTLE MOORINGS™ AND THE BEGINNERS BIBLE™

The Beginner's Bible
My Favorite Bible Stories

The people who brought you *The Beginner's Bible* proudly present *The Beginner's Bible My Favorite Bible Stories*. We invite you and your child to walk with us through the pages of this endearing collection of stories. We've assembled a sampling of our personal favorites. You and your child will enjoy these heart-warming stories brought to life through bright, full-color, kid-friendly illustrations. Discover the charm that made *The Beginner's Bible* a worldwide bestseller.

The Beginner's Bible
Read-Along Videos

Each *Beginner's Bible* read-along video is a nonanimated storybook video that brings to life the pages of *The Beginner's Bible* while encouraging your child to read along. Journey with us through the timeless stories and get to know the Bible characters favored by children young and old. A warm narration, fun and interesting characters, and enchanting music enhance your journey. Your child will love the kid-friendly illustrations from *The Beginner's Bible*. This video is available in Old and New Testament formats as well as a combination package.

The Beginner's Bible
Very First Adventures Series

These twenty-four-page books are designed in the classic storybook format. Each book introduces your child to a different adventure encountered by the characters from *The Beginner's Bible*.

NOAH SAVES THE ANIMALS
Imagine what it would be like to be asked to build a big boat and to load two of every kind of animal onto it. The animals and Noah's family must be saved from the flood. With God's help Noah can save the animals and his family. Come along and join the adventure as *Noah Saves the Animals*.

DAVID BRAVES THE GIANT
Imagine what it would be like to fight a mean giant when you are only a child. All the people were afraid of the giant. But not little David. With God's help David was not afraid. Come along and join the adventure as *David Braves the Giant*.